When Marcus Moore Moved In

Rebecca Bond

Megan Tingley Books
LITTLE, BROWN AND COMPANY
New York · An AOL Time Warner Company

Also by Rebecca Bond:

Just Like a Baby
Bravo, Maurice!

For Judy Sue, extraordinaire

First Edition

Library of Congress Cataloging-in-Publication Data

Bond, Rebecca.
  When Marcus Moore moved in / Rebecca Bond. — 1st ed.
    p. cm.
  Summary: Marcus is lonely on his first day in the new neighborhood, but then he makes
a good friend.
  ISBN 0-316-10458-2
  [1. Moving, Household—Fiction. 2. Friendship—Fiction.] I. Title.

PZ7.B63686 Wh 2003
[E]—dc21   2001038441

10 9 8 7 6 5 4 3 2 1

TWP

Printed in Singapore

The illustrations for this book were done in acrylic.
The text was set in Horley Old Style, and the display type was handlettered.

At 44 MacDougal Street when Marcus Moore moved in,
"I'm here!" said Marcus Moore,

but there was no one there.

There was no one coming up the street.

There was no one coming down.

There were only beds and boxes.

There were only rolls of rugs.

There was only early morning,

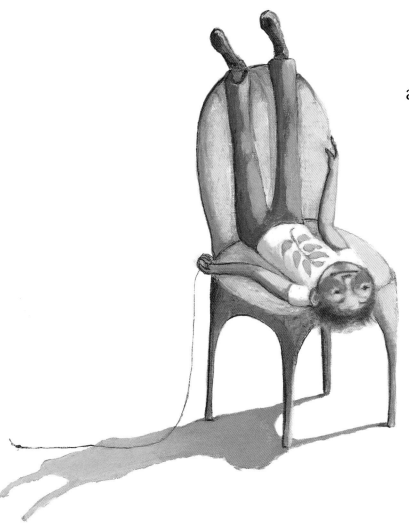

and there was only him,

at 44 MacDougal Street when Marcus Moore moved in.

Then *tap!* Ta-tap! Ta-tap!
Right beside his stoop,

like a sunny sidewalk dancer,
a girl went skipping by.

And *ringle! Jingle! Jangle!* There she was again.
With noisy bursts of music, she rang her bicycle bell.

She stomped   and tromped   and swaggered.

Ker-UNCH! Ker-UNCH! Ker-UNCH!

She lifted high her heels.
Ka-LOMP! Ka-LOMP! Ka-LOMP!

And BOOM-BA-DEE! BOOM-BA-DEE! BOOM-BA-DEE!
Like that she banged her drum,

at 44 MacDougal Street when Marcus Moore moved in.

"Wait!" cried Marcus Moore, but she was gone too fast.
    And the sky was turning dark,
    and it began to rain.

And there was only grim and gray, and there was only him,

at 44 MacDougal Street when Marcus Moore moved in.

Then *KNOCK! KNOCK! KNOCK!* "May I come in?" Marcus heard it clearly.

And she was at his doorway!
"Come in!" cried Marcus Moore.

"I'm Marcus Moore!" said Marcus Moore.
"I'm Katherine Brown!" said Kate.

And at once he felt all rosy. Like that, his street had changed,

beneath the *tic!*

and *tac-tac-tac!*

and *POUND! POUND! POUND!* of rain.
At 44 MacDougal Street when Marcus Moore moved in.

And all the afternoon that day, when the summer storm had ended,
they went *tap! Ta-tap! Ta-tapping* up and down the streets.

They went *ringle! Jingle! Jangle!*

And *ker-UNCH! Ker-UNCH! Ker-UNCH!*

They went *klomp! Ka-LOMP! Ka-LOMP*ing.

They went *BOOM-BA-DEE! BOOM-BA-DEE! BOOM!*

They stayed and played beneath the trees,

and over seas they sailed,

at 44 MacDougal Street when Marcus Moore moved in.

And in the early evening, when the day was blue and dusty,
with smells of dinners cooking, with lightly layered dark,

there were people coming up the street,
there were people coming down,

there were steps and stoops and sidewalks,
there were dogs and trucks and trees,

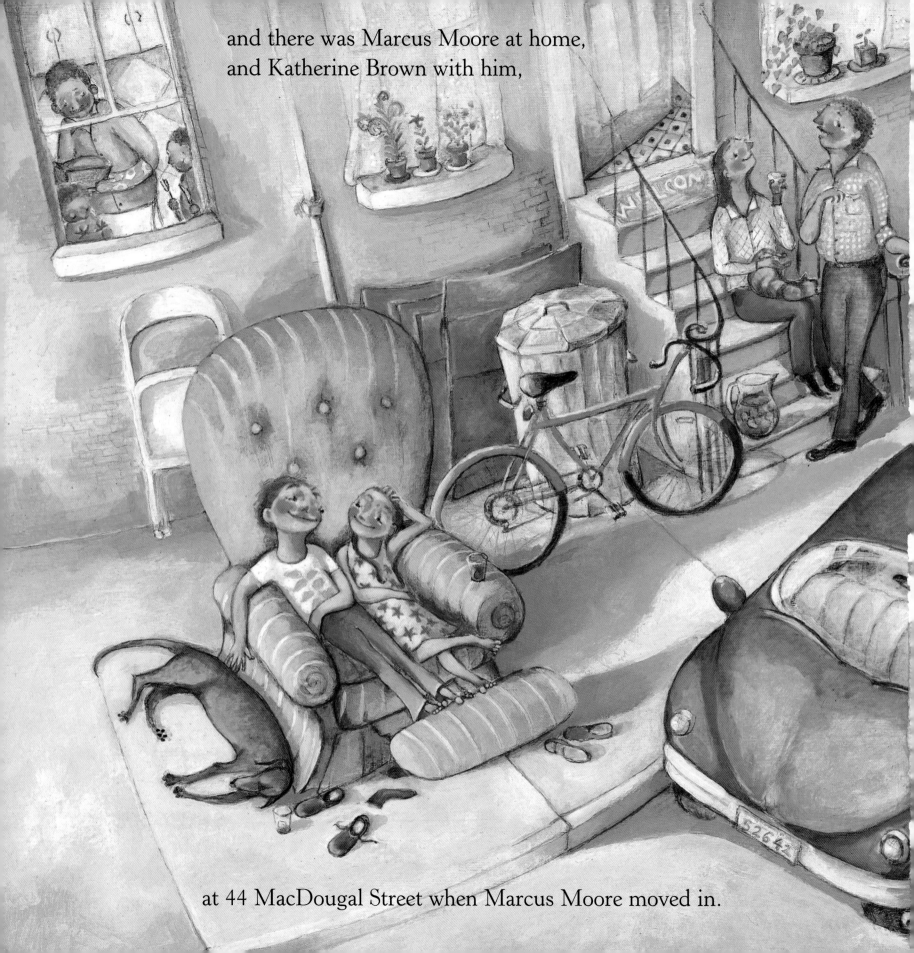

and there was Marcus Moore at home,
and Katherine Brown with him,

at 44 MacDougal Street when Marcus Moore moved in.